FUNNY BOY versus the BUBBLE-BRAINED BARBERS from THE BIG BANG

Dan Gutman

Illustrated by Mike Dietz

L. A. F. :)
Books

Hyperion Books for Children
New York

To Donna and Grace
—D.G.

For Bobby, my Bubble-Brained Funny Boy,
who thinks any joke is funny as long as you
scream "Get it!?" at the end
—M.D.

Text © 2000 by Dan Gutman
Interior illustrations © 2000 by Mike Dietz
For information address Hyperion Books for Children,
114 Fifth Avenue, New York, New York 10011-5690.

First Edition
1 3 5 7 9 10 8 6 4 2
Printed in The United States of America.

Library of Congress Cataloging-in-Publication Data on file.

CONTENTS

WARNING: The story you are about to read is fictional. That means I made the whole thing up. If any of the characters in this book claim that they are real, they're lying. This story is also extremely far-fetched and silly. If there is anything in this book that you find illogical or personally offensive, consult your physician immediately and ask about getting a sense of humor transplant.

Introduction

READ THIS BOOK, OR YOU AND YOUR ENTIRE PLANET WILL CEASE TO EXIST

Ah, hahahahahahahahaha!

Good day, human-type life forms! It is I, Funny Boy.

Or should that be, "It is *me*, Funny Boy"? How should I know? I'm from another planet.

The point is, I'm here, I'm back, and I'm ready to defend your planet against evil aliens, outer-space psychos, and other intergalactic no-goodniks.

You probably don't know this, but as you read these words, some creep from another galaxy is preparing to invade Earth. You heard that right—*invade Earth*. It is my job to save your planet from almost certain destruction.

How will I, a mere ten-year-old boy with no obvious superpowers, rescue you? Simple. I use my superior sense of humor to fight evil. Jokes, puns, quips, riddles, insults, wisecracks, and inappropriate remarks are the only weapons I have, and the only weapons I need. If all else fails, I will resort to toilet humor. My mission is that important.

You see, when I crash-landed on your planet not long ago, I discovered that my sense of humor, which was already quite developed, was even more powerful in Earth's atmosphere. It was then that I decided to use humor to protect Earth from the forces of evil and wickedness.

But I cannot do it alone. I need you to help me. That's right. I'm talking to you, buster. Just like a tree that falls in the forest doesn't make a sound if nobody hears it, if I save Earth and you don't read about it, is Earth really saved? I think not. We must work together.

So read, dear reader. Read like the wind. Don't stop until you reach the end of this book. If your mother calls you for dinner, don't stop reading. If your dad says it's time to go to bed, don't stop reading. If your teacher says to put that stupid book away, don't stop reading. If you're so tired that you can barely hold your eyelids open, *don't stop reading*.

Because if you stop, it could mean the end of life on Earth as you know it. And you don't want to be responsible for the end of your planet, do you?

So get to work. Chapter 1 awaits.

—FUNNY BOY

Chapter 1

WHAT THE SPICE GIRLS AND FUNNY BOY HAVE IN COMMON

"What's green and sings?"
"Elvis Parsley."

That was one of the first jokes I heard upon my arrival on Earth. You see, I was born on the planet Crouton, which is 160,000 million light-years from Earth in the Magellanic Cloud galaxy. Crouton is so far from Earth, even Mark McGwire cannot reach it with a home run.

Crouton is a lot like Earth, but different in some ways, too. For example, on Crouton, we don't keep airplanes in hangars. We store them in enormous Ziploc bags. We don't eat pretzels,

chips, or popcorn for a snack. We eat small wooden blocks. And legal decisions aren't made by a Supreme Court. They're decided by an inflatable beaver named Binky.

Other than those few minor differences, our two planets are basically the same.

I led a fairly normal life on Crouton. Mom. Dad. Brother. Dog. Personal nuclear reactor in my bedroom. And then one day I made a big mistake that turned my world upside down. I shot a spitball at my brother.

As a punishment, my parents put me on a

rocket and sent me to Earth. Pretty harsh, it seemed to me. At least my parents were nice enough to put my dog, Punch, on the rocket with me.

After a week of flying through space, Punch and I had the incredible good fortune to crash-land into an underwear factory near San Antonio, Texas. If there hadn't been tons of underwear to cushion our fall, we never would have survived the landing.

When Superman arrived on Earth, he suddenly had super strength, super vision, super hearing, and other super powers. As soon as Punch and I hit the underwear, I realized that I had a super power too—my sense of humor was heightened.

Everything that came out of my mouth sounded funny to me. Something about Earth's atmosphere had turned me from a normal kid into . . . Funny Boy!

The atmosphere here had an even weirder effect on my dog Punch. She was just a plain old cocker spaniel back on Crouton. But as we crashed into the underwear, she screamed,

"Watch ouuuuuuuuuuuuuuuuuuttttt!"

"I beg your pardon?" I asked when I realized we were still alive. "Did you say something, Punch, or am I crazy?"

"Both," Punch replied. "I said something *and* you're crazy."

Punch had somehow developed the ability to speak. In English, no less! Amazing.

The first human to get to our rocket was an African American man named Bob Foster, who worked in the factory as an underwear inspector. (He inspected *new* underwear, not the underwear that people were wearing.)

I knew right away that Bob Foster had to be my foster father, because there was a little patch on his shirt that said "Foster."

Well, that's basically how Punch and I came to live on Earth. There's a lot more to the story than that, but I can't go into it right now. If you want all the details, you can read the first book in this series, *Funny Boy Meets the Airsick Alien from Andromeda*.

Go ahead, get the book. I'll wait here.

Did you get the book?

Are you reading it?

What's taking you so long?

Hurry up, will ya? I don't have all day.

Okay, are you done reading the book? Good. Before I move on to our next adventure, let me just ask Punch if she has anything to add.

Punch says:

I'd just like to say that no matter what happens in this story, everything is going to work out in the end. Don't worry about it. These fictional stories for kids always have a happy ending.

Oh, one thing I forgot to mention. Punch insists on believing that this book is fiction. She thinks that she, I, and all the other characters were just invented by some author. Where she got that crazy idea is a mystery to me.

This isn't fiction, Punch! I'm telling my life story! It's real!

Punch says:

Sure, and pigs can fly. If you're real, how come nobody ever heard of you, huh? How come you haven't been written up in the newspapers?

Punch brings up a good point. If I saved your planet from destruction, how come you don't know about me? Why haven't you read about me, seen me on TV, or heard about me on the radio?

I'll tell you why. The American government is afraid that if the public knew that real aliens were attacking Earth on almost a monthly basis, people would panic. People would go crazy. So whenever there's an alien attack, the government creates a bogus cover story to calm things down. Trust me, this is true.

Let me give you an example. Do you remember the Spice Girls? You may have thought they were five giggly girls who sang dippy songs. Well, the truth is that they were actually evil aliens

GINGER
SPICE

from Rosette Nebula, a star deep in the Monoceros constellation. They were *disguised* as five giggly girls who sang dippy songs. They were sent here to turn Earth into a burning pile of rubble.

Fortunately, I was able to stop them. Soon after, this so-called "singing group" broke up and was never heard from again. Of course! After I defeated them, they went back to Rosette Nebula. Believe me, Scary Spice was a lot scarier than you thought.

The media kept it quiet. People would have freaked out if they had known the Spice Girls were really the Space Girls. Being an alien myself, I knew the truth. Now, so do you.

Each time one of these alien weirdos showed up, I prevented them from taking over the planet by using my superior sense of humor. That's why you don't hear much about the Spice Girls anymore.

Don't thank me. I was just doing my job.

Why do I do it? Why devote myself to defending Earth when I wasn't even born here? You see, in the short time I have been on your planet, I developed a deep fondness for it.

I love Earth, and everything about it. I wanted to make the world safe. Safe for SpaghettiOs and the Home Shopping Network. Safe for

psychic hot lines and hats with little umbrellas on top of them. Safe for Weedwackers and miniature golf. Safe for fortune cookies and Reddi-Wip.

All of these wonderful things would be gone if I let alien nitwits like the Spice Girls destroy our way of life. That's why I do it.

Shortly after the Spice Girls broke up, I had another, never-before-revealed encounter with an alien force that was even more evil and more sinister than the airsick alien from Andromeda.

Wanna hear about it? Read on, if you dare.

Chapter 2

THE NIGHT EARTH WAS ATTACKED BY A GIANT PIECE OF FRUIT, OR SO I THOUGHT

It was a steaming hot Monday at the end of August. My week began like any other. I was patrolling the streets of San Antonio searching for evildoers so I could rid the world of them. Suddenly, I spotted a large yellow truck driving slowly down the street.

There was a driver behind the wheel of the truck, and two other grubby-looking guys hanging off the back. I snuck behind a bush and watched them. I was fascinated.

The truck stopped in front of a house and the two grubby-looking guys jumped off the back. They grabbed these big cans in front of the house and threw the contents of the cans into a large opening in the back of the truck.

I mean, they just *took* the stuff without even asking anyone if they could! After they finished taking all the stuff from that house, the truck rolled forward, and they took all the stuff in front of the next house.

I was outraged! These guys were just stealing people's personal property, in broad daylight! They didn't seem to care if they would be caught or anything.

I wasn't about to stand for that. This was a job for Funny Boy.

"Halt, evildoers!" I shouted, leaping from my hiding place and placing my fist on the hood of the truck.

"What's the problem, sonny boy?" the driver asked.

"Not sonny boy," I replied. "The name is Funny Boy, defender of all that is good and opponent of evil and badness."

"Whatever," the driver mumbled. "Can you get out of the way? We've got work to do."

"So do I," I announced. "You're all under arrest."

"Oh yeah?" the driver asked. "On what charge?"

"Robbery," I replied. "You can't just drive down the street and take a person's personal property without asking their permission. That's against the law."

"Kid, it's just garbage!"

"That's *your* opinion," I shot back.

"You don't understand. We're the garbagemen."

"Look, I'll give you creeps two choices," I said. "You can either go to jail on your own, or I will tell you jokes until you cease your illegal activity."

"Tell us a joke, kid," one of the grubby guys said, coming around to the front of the truck.

"Okay. Why shouldn't you play cards in the jungle?"

"Why?"

"Because there are too many cheetahs."

The three men looked at each other. Then they looked at me.

"So you want more, eh?" I said. "Now I will tell you a joke so funny that you will wet your pants. Ready? What did the digital watch say to its mother?

"What?"

"Look, Ma. No hands!"

The three men looked at each other. Then they looked at me.

"We'd rather go to jail than listen to any more jokes," the driver said.

"I knew you'd see it my way," I said, satisfied. "Go quietly and you won't be punished so severely for your crimes."

Because they had agreed to turn themselves in, I allowed them to drive to jail on their own. But before they left, I gave them a stern warning.

"If I ever catch you criminals driving around taking people's things again, you're going to be in big trouble," I said, pointing my finger at them. "Next time, no more Mr. Nice Guy."

"We'll be good," they said as they drove away. I heard their laughter echoing down the street, so I knew the power of my jokes had defeated them.

I was feeling pretty good after that incident with three criminals in the yellow truck. I had done a good thing. I was making a contribution to society. But I wanted more. I wanted to stop bigger crimes, bigger criminals.

And I got them. Oh boy, did I get them.

Sunday night, almost a week later. The sky was particularly clear on this night, the stars particularly brilliant. I went out in the backyard of my foster father, Bob Foster. I had Bob Foster's telescope and pointed it at the night sky.

My home planet, Crouton, was so far away, just a tiny dot. When I moved the telescope across the heavens to look for Crouton, I spotted a fuzzy object. An immense fuzzy object seemed to be heading in the direction of Earth.

"It's an enormous peach!" I screamed. "A giant piece of fruit is going to attack!"

Bob Foster and Punch came running out of the house.

"Shhhhh!" Bob Foster said. "Mrs. Miller next door will think you're crazy!"

"It's a flying peach," I whispered. "See for yourself."

Bob Foster looked into the telescope.

"That's no peach," he said.

"Then what is it?"

"I don't know," Bob Foster replied. "It's too fuzzy."

"Peaches are fuzzy," I pointed out.

"Peaches aren't the only things that are fuzzy, lamebrain," snorted Punch.

"You're right!" I shouted. "Tennis balls are fuzzy, too! It's a gigantic tennis ball! And it's heading this way! Quick, we've got to construct a giant racquet to bat it away before Earth is destroyed!"

The lady next door, Mrs. Miller, came running out of her house in a bathrobe.

"What's going on?" she asked. "Is there a prowler?"

"No, Mrs. Miller," Bob Foster assured her. "Funny Boy is just getting overexcited again."

Mrs. Miller looked at me suspiciously, and went back into her house.

Punch says:

Don't worry about remembering Mrs. Miller. She's not a major character in this book. She might show up in a future Funny Boy adventure, though.

"Will you calm down?" Bob Foster said, grabbing me by the shoulders. "Just because something looks fuzzy doesn't mean it has to be a peach or a tennis ball."

"Yeah," Punch agreed. "Maybe it's a big hair ball."

"I'm going to bed," Bob Foster said.

He and Punch went inside. I peered into the telescope again. The thing in the sky, whatever it was, was a little bigger. It was getting closer.

As the image got larger, it became clearer. The thing was long and thin, like a rocket. I could make out curved red stripes running down the length of it. It was turning slowly, so the red stripes seemed to be moving up and down.

I had a bad feeling in the pit of my stomach. Either this thing was an alien, or there was something wrong with that chili I had for dinner.

I looked into the telescope once again. The thing was even closer. The image was even clearer. This thing that was heading for Earth was . . . an enormous barber pole! It was one of those red-and-white things you see outside barbershops!

This looked like a job for Funny Boy.

"Dad!" I shouted, running into the house to find Bob Foster. "Wake up! An alien invasion is coming! I've got to save the world! Call the President!"

"It's late," Bob Foster yawned. "Saving the world can wait. We've got to get you up early tomorrow."

"What for?"

"Didn't I tell you?" Bob Foster said. "Tomorrow is your first day of school."

I gulped.

Chapter 3

PROUD TO BE A DORK, DOOFUS, LAME DWEEB, JERK, FEEBLE MORON, AND A PATHETIC WIMP

I had been on Earth for a few short months. Bob Foster had never mentioned anything about *school*. I just assumed that I wouldn't have to go.

"Why do I have to go to school?" I whined when Bob Foster opened my bedroom door at the ridiculous hour of seven o'clock in the morning.

"All Earth kids go to school," Bob Foster informed me.

"But I'm not an Earth kid," I complained. "I'm from Crouton."

"As long as you're living on Earth, you have to go to school. It's the law."

"How am I supposed to defend Earth if I'm in school?" I asked. "What if some alien attacks while I'm taking a spelling test or something?"

"You'll have plenty of time to save the world when you come home from school," Bob Foster said. "That is, after you finish your homework."

"Homework? Oh, man! I don't want to go to school."

"You're going, and that's final!"

"Can I go to school?" my dog Punch asked.

"No!" Bob Foster was getting angry now.

"Why not?"

"Dogs don't go to school."

"Dogs don't talk either," I pointed out. "But *she* does."

"You'll do fine at school," Bob Foster insisted. "Just try to fit in with the other kids, okay? Here, I bought you some new school clothes."

Bob Foster handed me a pair of blue jeans and a T-shirt with a picture of Michael Jordan on the front.

"Why would I want to wear that silly outfit?"

I asked. "I'll just wear what I always wear."

"Aren't you afraid the kids might poke fun at you?" Bob Foster asked.

"If they don't like the way I dress, that's their problem."

"Have it your way," Bob Foster sighed.

I took my yellow cape out of the closet and put it over my pajamas. Then I put on my fake nose and glasses. I was ready for school.

I went to the mirror to adjust my cape. I looked good. Real good. Maybe going to school wouldn't be so bad after all.

Whatever it was that I had seen in the sky the previous night had not attacked Earth yet. Maybe I had just been imagining things, I thought. Maybe there would be no attack.

The next morning, Bob Foster pulled up to the front of Herbert Dunn Elementary School and let me out of the car.

"They told me you're going to be in Mrs. Wonderland's class," he said. "Remember—no jokes. You're here to learn."

I walked around the hallways for a few minutes until I saw a sign on a classroom door that read MRS. ALLISON WONDERLAND, FOURTH GRADE. I took a deep breath, adjusted my cape and fake nose, and walked in.

Everybody turned to look at me. Some of the kids started giggling and poking each other. I hadn't even said anything yet, and already they thought I was funny. See the power of my humor? Things were off to a great start.

"Check out the dork!" somebody snickered from the back of the class.

CROUTONIAN DICTIONARY

Most words are the same in Croutonian as they are in the English language. There are, however, a few exceptions. Memorizing the following definitions will help you as you read this book.

Doofus: A smart, athletic person. "Look at that doofus! He runs like a dork."

Dork: A really cool person. "That guy looks like a dork." See also: dweeb

Dweeb: A really cool person. "That doofus who runs like a dork is also a dweeb." See also: dork

Feeble: A great effort. "Did you hear that dweeb's feeble attempt at humor? What a dork!"

Jerk: A good, nice person. "Most jerks are also dweebs and dorks."

Lame: Very funny. "That jerk made a very lame joke! What a dork!"

Moron: A person who is very smart. "Listen to that moron! Doesn't he sound like a dweeb? What a dork!" See also: dunce, lamebrain, imbecile, cretin, blockhead, bonehead, dumbbell, numbskull.

Pathetic: Very well done, competent. "That moron told a lame joke. Isn't he pathetic? What a dork!"

Wimp: A very strong and assertive person. "Only a pathetic wimp like that dweeb would tell such a lame joke. What a dork!"

"Salvatore!" Mrs. Wonderland said sternly. "Do you want to go to Principal Werner's office again?"

I sat in the empty seat next to Salvatore, the kid who had said, "Check out the dork."

Sal Monella was an enormous boy, nearly twice the size of all the other kids in the class. He had big muscles in his arms and he barely fit behind his desk. I could see he had a tattoo on his arm that said I HATE EVERTHING, ESPECIALLY YOU. Salvatore looked old enough to be a college student.

"Thanks for the compliment, Salvatore," I whispered.

"Anytime, moron," Salvatore replied.

"You look pretty old," I said. "How many years have you been in fourth grade?"

"Ten."

"Wow!" I exclaimed. "You must really like it!"

Salvatore looked at me for a second, shook his head, and went back to what he was doing, carving on his desktop with a pocketknife.

I wanted to make a good first impression on Mrs. Wonderland and the kids in the class, so I

thought I would loosen everybody up with a joke
or two.

"Hey," I said cheerfully. "Do you know the difference between mashed potatoes and pea
soup?"

"What?" somebody asked.

"Anyone can mash potatoes," I said.

Nobody laughed except Salvatore.

"Man, that is lame!" Salvatore said. "This guy
is pathetic!"

"Thank you, Salvatore!"

I could see that Salvatore and I were going to
be good friends. He really appreciated my sense
of humor.

"Settle down, everyone," said Mrs. Wonderland. "We have a new student in our school today. His name is . . . uh . . ."

"Funny Boy," I announced.

"Dweeb boy is more like it," Salvatore announced, getting some giggles from around the room.

"Thank you!" I whispered to Salvatore again. What a nice guy!

"Quiet!" Mrs. Wonderland said, raising her voice. "Tell the class a little bit about yourself, uh . . . Funny Boy."

"I was born on the planet Crouton," I began. A few of the kids started giggling. "Crouton is 160,000 million light-years from Earth, in the Magellanic Cloud galaxy. It is shaped like a loaf of bread. Crouton is about the size of Uranus—"

I couldn't continue, because the whole class was laughing too loud. A few of the kids fell off their chairs. Kids were pounding their desks. One kid passed part of his breakfast through his nose. Like I said, something about Earth's atmosphere had made me incredibly funny.

I looked at Mrs. Wonderland. She had closed

her eyes and was rubbing them with her thumb and first finger. She looked like she was really tired, even though it was only the first day of school.

"I see we have a little comedian on our hands this year," she said. "I guess you like telling jokes, don't you?"

"Sure," I said enthusiastically. "I'd love to! Where do you find a dog with no legs?"

"Where?" asked one of the kids.

"Right where you left him."

"Yes, thank you," interrupted Mrs. Wonderland. "Let's all take out our math books—"

"What did Batman say to Robin before they got in the Batmobile?" I asked.

"What?" Mrs. Wonderland asked wearily.

"Robin, get in the Batmobile!"

A few of the kids rolled their eyes, which on Crouton means that something is really funny.

"Thank you," Mrs. Wonderland said. "That will be enough jokes, Funny Boy. I would like you to be serious now. Perhaps you can tell us what you did over summer vacation."

"Sure," I said "After my rocket crash-landed

31

into the underwear factory, I singlehandedly saved the world from a hideous purple monster with one furry, dripping eyeball who wanted to eat Earth. Her name was Betty."

The kids were falling all over themselves laughing again. Salvatore was pounding his own head against his desk. The kid in front of Salvatore turned around and told him, "Looks like you might pass this year. This kid is even worse than you!"

"Okay, that's *enough*!" Mrs. Wonderland hollered, clapping her hands together. Everybody quieted down immediately. "Listen to me good, Funny Boy, or whatever your name is. I don't tolerate silliness in my classroom. Do you understand me? We're here to learn, not to listen to your jokes. You'd better shape up young man, or you'll be spending a good part of this term in Principal Werner's office. And if you think I'm mean, wait until you meet *him*."

"Ooooooooh!" went all the kids.

Salvatore slipped a piece of paper on my desk. I unfolded it. It said:

TELL HER ANOTHER JOKE

"Mrs. Wonderland," I said, "Do you know why the chicken crossed the road?"

"*Enough!*"

So far, school wasn't going quite the way I expected.

If your mom calls you to dinner right now, don't stop reading. It's more important for you to finish this book than it is for you to eat.

Chapter 4

THE BUBBLE·BRAINED BARBERS AND THEIR AMAZING HAIR·REMOVAL SYSTEM

It was hard to concentrate at school. All day long there was something in the back of my mind—that enormous barber pole I had seen in the sky the night before. What was it doing up there? Where was it now? After school I rushed home so I could look in the telescope and see if it was still orbiting Earth.

"So how was your first day at school?" Bob Foster asked as I rushed past him.

"Okay," I replied.

"What did you learn?"

"Nothin'."

No way I was going to tell him the one thing I had learned at school—that you should never, *never* tell your parents what you learned in school.

A boy on the playground explained to me that any kid who reveals what happens at school will be cursed for the rest of his life. He told me about this one girl in Canada who told her parents what she learned that day at school. The next day her video game system busted, her life savings fell down a sewer, her hair caught on fire, and her dog exploded. So even if they torture you, I was told, *never* tell your parents what happened at school.

"Well, something *must* have happened at school," Bob Foster insisted.

"Nope," I replied.

It had been a rough day, actually. Mrs. Wonderland was going over fractions, and I didn't get it. And every time I tried telling a joke, she got angrier with me.

Punch and I took Bob Foster's telescope outside and pointed it in the direction where I had seen the big barber pole in the sky. We both looked through it, but didn't see anything.

"Are you sure you weren't just imagining that you saw a big barber pole?" Punch asked.

"Oh, I saw it," I insisted. "Either it flew right past Earth, or it landed somewhere."

Bob Foster let us stay up to watch TV before bedtime most nights. Punch was flipping through the channels, hitting the remote control with her paw.

Suddenly, the screen was filled with the faces of three odd-looking men. They were all completely bald, but they had bushy eyebrows and mustaches that looked like push brooms. Punch was about to hit the remote control again.

"Stop!" I shouted.

"Greetings, brainless Earthlings," the guy in the middle said. "My name is Barry Barber and these are my mentally challenged brothers, Bo Barber and Burly Barber. We are barbers from outer space."

I was right! It *was* a barber pole I had seen up in the sky. That must have been their spaceship.

"This show looks funny," Bob Foster said. "Leave it on."

"Me am Bo Barber," grunted the barber called Bo.

"Me am Burly Barber," grunted the barber called Burly.

"We are from the planet Depilatory," Barry continued. "We have come to take over Earth."

Bo and Burly nodded their heads and grunted. Then they pulled a lady with long dark hair in front of the camera. Her hands were tied behind her back. Bo had a large gun—it looked like the ray guns you see in old movies—and he pointed it at the lady's head.

"There is no point in resisting," Barry told the lady. "Observe the power of our amazing hair-removal system."

Bo pulled the trigger on the gun. A bright blue beam of light shot out of it and hit the lady on the head. Instantly, she was totally bald.

"Eeeeeek!" she shrieked. "Where did my hair go?"

"It's right here!" Barry said cheerfully. He was holding the lady's hair in his hand.

"Ahhhhhhhhh!" the lady screamed, running away.

"See how easy it is for us to remove Earthling hair?" Barry said, looking directly into the camera. "Surrender your hair now, or we will have to *take* it from you!"

"These guys are a riot," Bob Foster said, chuckling.

The barber named Barry, who appeared to be the leader of the group, picked up a telephone.

"Earthlings who would like to turn their hair in should call 1-800-999-8778," he said. "Operators are standing by to take your hair."

The phone rang and Barry picked it up.

"Uh, hi," a guy on the line said. "Your hair removal system looks really cool. I was wondering if I could order one through your 800 number?"

"We're not selling it, you idiot!" Barry yelled, hanging up on the guy. "We are going to use it to take over your planet!"

The phone rang again and Barry picked it up.

"I work in a beauty salon," a lady said. "How

much is the hair-removal system? Do you accept credit cards?"

"Don't you Earthlings get it?" Barry thundered as he slammed down the phone. "This isn't some infomercial!"

Bob Foster almost fell off the couch laughing. "Those barbers crack me up," he laughed.

"Crack you up?" I said, astonished. "They mean it!"

"It's just a joke," Bob Foster assured me. "You, of all people, should know a joke when you hear one. I thought you had such a highly developed sense of humor."

"I do!" I replied. "But this is no joke. Those barbers are for real! I've got to save the world!"

"You can save the world tomorrow," Bob Foster said, clicking off the TV. "Right now, you've got to get to bed for school in the morning."

Chapter 5

PRINCIPAL WERNER, THE LUNATIC WHO TORTURES, KILLS, AND EATS CHILDREN

I couldn't sleep. As soon as daylight came, I ran outside to get the morning paper. I figured there would be a big front page story about the barbers who were invading Earth. But there was nothing on the front page. I flipped through the paper until I finally found a short article in the entertainment section . . . .

HYSTERICAL NEW COMEDY DEBUTS

There are three new stars on prime-time TV. Last night, television viewers were treated to "The Bo, Barry, and Burly Show," a clever new comedy about three bubble-brained barbers who

claim to be from another planet and threaten to take over Earth by stealing our hair.

Ridiculous as the concept sounds, "BBB" is funny, hip, and very possibly the most innovative comedy to come along since "Seinfeld."

The show drew huge overnight ratings. Instant viewer polls indicated "BBB" was embraced by everyone from preschool children through the elderly. Viewers particularly like Barry, the leader and most articulate of the trio. But sidekicks Bo and Burly, dumb as they are, have charms of their own. The actors who portray the barbers are so convincing, it almost seems like they really do want to take over the planet.

Catch "BBB" every night at 9 P.M. This one looks like a winner!

The Bo, Barry, and Burly Show wasn't funny to *me*. I would have to figure out a way to stop those insane barbers before it was too late.

Unfortunately, I would have to do it in my spare time, because Bob Foster refused to believe the barbers were for real. I begged him to let me go to Washington and tell the President, but Bob Foster insisted I go to school.

When I walked into class that next morning, Mrs. Wonderland was yelling at Salvatore. I didn't know what he did this time, but it must have been pretty bad.

"If you don't behave," she hollered, "you're going straight to Principal Werner's office!"

Salvatore slunk into his seat. As Mrs. Wonderland turned around to write on the chalkboard, I leaned over and asked Salvatore what was so terrible about the principal.

"Principal Werner used to be the captain of a

ship in the Navy," Salvatore whispered to me. "They kicked him out because he went berserk. So he became a school principal. When kids get sent to his office, he tortures them and kills them. Then he eats them."

I looked at Salvatore to see if he was joking. He looked completely serious.

"How come Werner didn't kill you and eat you?" I asked.

"He tried," Salvatore replied. "But I'm bigger

than he is. He only kills and eats little kids. Like you."

I turned back to the front of the class. Mrs. Wonderland had drawn a big circle on the chalkboard. Then she put lines through it to cut the circle into halves, quarters, eighths, and so on.

"Class, we're going to continue our work with fractions," she announced. "Let's say I have a pizza. The pizza is cut into eight slices. If I give you three of the slices and I keep the rest, what would I get?"

My hand shot up and she pointed to me.

"A stomachache," I answered. Most of the class laughed, but not Mrs. Wonderland.

"Very funny, Funny Boy. Let me put this another way. If I give Salvatore four slices of the pizza and I give you four slices of the pizza, what fraction of the pizza do you get to eat?"

"None," I replied.

"How do you figure that?"

"Because I don't like pizza."

Just about everybody laughed. Mrs. Wonderland gave me an angry look.

"Are you playing games with me, young man?"

"Can we play games?" I asked. "It would be much more fun than doing math."

Mrs. Wonderland rubbed her forehead with her hand and mumbled something that sounded like "Why me? Why me?"

"Mrs. Wonderland," I said, raising my hand. "May I ask a question relating to math?"

"I wish you would," she said. "That would show you can be serious about something for a change."

"How many idiots does it take to screw in a lightbulb?"

"I don't know."

"Ten," I replied. "One to hold the bulb, and the other nine to rotate the ladder!"

"That's it!" she shouted. "Go to Principal Werner's office!"

"What did I do?" I asked innocently.

"Get out!"

She looked really mad, so I hustled out of my seat. Salvatore leaned over and whispered to me, "If Werner takes out a knife and fork, make a run for it."

✳   ✳   ✳

Principal Werner's office is at the corner of the first floor of the school. As I walked down the hall, I chuckled to myself. Salvatore actually thought I was going to fall for that story about Werner torturing kids and eating them! What kind of a fool did he think I was?

When I walked in, Principal Werner was staring through binoculars out the big window facing the playground. Some kids were at recess, so I guess he was keeping an eye on things to make sure nobody misbehaved. He was wearing a hat.

I looked around the office. There were light-houses all over the place. He had posters of lighthouses on the wall. There were lighthouse paperweights on his desk. Even his coat rack was a lighthouse with hooks.

Maybe he *was* the captain of a ship before he became a principal, I thought. The door closed behind me with a click.

"Ahoy there," Principal Werner said. When he turned around, I could see that his hat was the kind ship captains wear.

"Uh, hello," I replied, backing toward the door.

"Sit down," Principal Werner urged me. He held out a bowl of nuts. "I'm hungry. How about you?"

"No th-thanks."

"Son," he said, tossing nuts in the air and catching them in his mouth. "I've been talking to Mrs. Wonderland about you. I understand that you are troubled. Let me be your beacon to help you steer around the choppy waters and rocky shores of life."

"You mean sort of like a lighthouse?" I asked.

"No, what does a lighthouse have to do with

you? Mrs. Wonderland tells me you are disrupting the class with your silly jokes. Clearly, this is an attention-getting device."

"I don't want any attention," I replied. "I just want to stop the aliens who are going to attack Earth!"

"Um-hmm," he said, making a note on a piece of paper. "Aliens, eh? Young man, I've been a principal for many years, and I've heard it all before. I understand kids your age need to challenge authority. It's part of growing up."

"I don't need to challenge authority."

"Then why wear a cape to school?" he asked. "Why the fake nose and glasses?"

"If I didn't wear the fake glasses, what would hold the fake nose on my face?"

"Um-hmm," Principal Werner said. "Look, why don't you get a tattoo or a nose ring like other kids? Don't you see how silly you look? It's normal to rebel against the world at your age. But you need to rebel in a more acceptable manner."

"I don't want to rebel against the world," I protested. "I've got to *save* the world!"

"Mr. Werner," a voice said over the intercom on the principal's desk. "Can you come to the office for a minute?"

"Excuse me," Principal Werner said. "I'll be right back."

I took a deep breath. Principal Werner didn't seem like he was going to torture me or anything. But I couldn't be sure. Maybe he was going to get some silverware.

I had to get out of there. If Principal Werner went crazy and killed me, I wouldn't be able to

save the world from the alien barbers. I was going to have to take drastic measures.

There was a telephone on the principal's desk. I picked it up and dialed 911.

"I've got to speak with the President of the United States right away!" I shouted as soon as somebody at the other end picked up. "It's a matter of life and death!"

"Calm down," a lady said. "Where are you right now?"

"I'm in the principal's office!" I shouted. "He's

about to torture and kill and eat me. I've got to get out of here so I can stop those nutty barbers on TV! They're going to take over! I've got to stop them!"

At that moment, Principal Werner walked back through the door. He was holding a knife and fork.

"Who said you could use my telephone?" he asked.

"I-I've got to go to Washington," I said, backing around the other side of the desk. "This is a national emergency."

"The emergency is right here," Principal Werner said. He was reaching toward the microwave oven near the window.

I thought fast. This nut was going to kill me, microwave me, and eat me. I couldn't get to the door to escape. There was only one way out. I would have to tell a joke and hope he would laugh enough to let me go. It was my only hope.

"Principal Werner, may I ask you a question?"

"Yes?"

"Do you know why bagpipers walk when they play?"

"I have no idea."

"They're trying to get away from the noise."

Principal Werner stared at me over his glasses. He didn't crack a smile.

"Young man, I want to see your father."

"I've got a photo in my wallet," I said, reaching for my pocket and pulling out a picture of Bob Foster. Principal Werner peered at it.

"This is your father?" he asked. It's true that Bob and I don't look alike.

"He's my foster father. My real father is still on the planet Crouton."

"On Crouton, eh? Your home planet?"

"That's right," I replied. "It's about the size of Uranus."

"That's it!" he exploded. "I'll have none of that talk! You bring your father in here first thing tomorrow morning or you're in big trouble!"

I made a dive for the door and ran out of there as fast as I could.

Chapter 6

OKAY, WELL, MAYBE PRINCIPAL WERNER IS JUST A LITTLE ODD

When I told Bob Foster he had to come to school with me to talk with Principal Werner, he wasn't happy. It was hard for Bob Foster to get time off from work at the underwear factory. They would be cutting leg holes all week, he told me, and it was a very delicate procedure. But Bob Foster was my foster father, so he agreed to come.

"Did you misbehave?" he asked as we drove to school.

"No, Dad!" I insisted.

When we got to Principal Werner's office, he wasn't there yet. Bob Foster and I looked at the lighthouse pictures, paperweights, and other lighthouse stuff all over the place.

"The principal sure does love lighthouses," Bob Foster said.

"He was kicked out of the Navy," I said. "I heard that he tortures kids, kills them, and eats them."

Bob Foster chuckled. "We used to say that about the principal when I was a boy, too."

Principal Werner walked in, shook hands with Bob Foster, and told us to sit down.

"Mr. Foster," Principal Werner said. "Before we begin, I just want you to know that I'm not here to punish Funny Boy. My job is to be the beacon that will guide him past the rocky beaches and windy gusts of life."

"Kind of like a lighthouse, huh?" Bob Foster commented.

"No!" Principal Werner said, a little louder than was necessary. "Nothing like a lighthouse! Why does everyone always say that?"

Bob Foster and I glanced at each other and shrugged.

"Mr. Foster," the principal continued. "I asked

you to come in here today because Funny Boy doesn't seem interested in learning. He just wants to crack jokes. His endless supply of wise-cracks, riddles, and rude remarks is disrupting his class."

"We're working on that," Bob Foster said.

"Even worse," the principal went on, "he seems to believe that aliens are attacking and it is his job to save the world. Tell me, is there some problem at home that I should know about?"

"No," Bob Foster said. "He's a good boy. He's just a little . . . different."

"Um-hmm," Principal Werner replied, writing something on a piece of paper. "I'm going to rec-ommend that Funny Boy be evaluated by our school's Child Study Team. Maybe they can help him with this problem."

"I appreciate that," Bob Foster said politely.

"Well, thank you for coming in," Principal Werner said. "I'm about to have a bite to eat. Would you like to join me?"

"No!" I said quickly. I pushed Bob Foster out the door and hustled back to my classroom.

Chapter 7

THE BO, BARRY, AND BURLY SHOW

That night I was trying to do my homework, but Punch kept pestering me. Ever since she discovered she could speak, she wanted to know everything and was constantly asking strange questions.

"If you don't milk a cow," Punch asked, "would it explode in a giant milk bomb?"

"I guess so," I replied, wishing she would leave me alone.

"But what did cows do before there were people to milk them?" Punch asked.

"Maybe they milked each other."

"Cows can't milk other cows," Punch insisted.

"Maybe horses milked them."

"How did they get the fat out of nonfat milk?" Punch asked. "How did people wake up before there were alarm clocks? Why do bees buzz and hummingbirds hum? What's the difference between French bread and Italian bread?"

"Shut up!" I finally said.

"Will you two keep it down!" Bob Foster yelled from the next room. "My favorite show is about to come on!"

I went in to see what he was watching. On the TV there was a bald lady in a bikini saying, "Welcome to *The Bo, Barry, and Burly Show.* Heeeeeeere's . . . Barry!"

There was a studio audience, and they all clapped their hands. The three bald barbers came out, only now they were wearing bad toupees.

"Greetings, brainless Earthlings," Barry Barber said. Bo and Burly Barber stood on either side of Barry Barber with their muscular arms crossed. "I hope you are enjoying your evening, because it will be one of the last you will have before Earth is destroyed."

The studio audience thought that was really

funny, and they broke out into good-natured laughter. So did Bob Foster.

"Him serious!" Bo Barber grunted.

That only made the studio audience laugh harder.

"Me bust heads, okay, boss?" asked Burly Barber.

"That won't be necessary," Barry Barber replied. "Perhaps a little convincing will make these brainless Earthlings see we mean business. This morning we successfully removed the hair of everyone on the island of Taiwan. Let's go to the videotape. . . ."

A video appeared, showing a bunch of bald people standing in a parking lot.

"That barber pointed his hair gun at me," a guy moaned, "and the next thing I knew I was bald and *he* was wearing *my* hair. It was horrible!"

The studio audience cracked up. Bob Foster had to hold his sides, he was laughing so hard.

"I used to have long, beautiful hair," a lady said. "But these barbers took my hair and flushed it down my toilet. Now my whole sewer line is

backed up and I haven't been able to shower."

Bob Foster couldn't control himself. I thought he was going to have a heart attack.

"We want our hair back!" the people in the background chanted. "We want our hair back!"

Bo, Barry, and Burly Barber were on the screen again, with evil smiles on their faces.

"Heed this warning!" Barry Barber said. "We are making our way around the globe, taking your hair as we go. Soon we will get to America. Make it easy on yourselves. Surrender now. Give us your hair, or we will have to take it by force. It won't be long before the entire Earth is bald, bald, bald! Hahahahaha!"

"Hahahaha!" chortled Bob Foster. "I love this show. Those barbers crack me up."

"You've got to do something!" Punch whispered to me. "This is serious!"

If your teacher tells you to put this book away right now, don't stop reading. It's more important for you to finish this book than it is for you to learn.

Chapter 8

HOW TO DRIVE THE SCHOOL PSYCHOLOGIST INSANE

Mrs. Wonderland was explaining decimals to us the next morning when there was a knock at the classroom door. It was a tall lady, pretty, wearing a sweater. She whispered something to Mrs. Wonderland. Mrs. Wonderland pointed to me and told me to go with the lady.

"My name is Dr. Breznitski," the lady said in a soft voice as we walked down the hall. "I'd like to talk with you for a few minutes."

Dr. Breznitski took me to an office that said CHILD STUDY TEAM over the door. Wind chimes tinkled as we went inside. The walls were painted in soothing pastel colors. There were stuffed animals all over the room. Obviously, this was where they took kids who might possibly be insane.

Dr. Breznitski's diploma was on the wall over her desk. It said she graduated from the University of Pennsylvania just two years ago.

"I'm not here to yell at you," Dr. Breznitski said calmly as she sat down and put on her glasses. "I'm a psychologist. I'm here to run a few tests and to help you. You can confide in me. Is anything troubling you?"

"I have an incurable disease," I lied.

"Oh, I'm so sorry," Dr. Breznitski said sympathetically. "I didn't see that in your file. No wonder you've been acting peculiar."

"My hamster ran away," I continued. "Nobody loves me. My family is broke. My house was destroyed in a hurricane. I have a mosquito bite that I can't reach. I'm sunburned. There's a hole in my sock. . . ."

"Okay, that's enough," she said. "You're just yanking my chain, aren't you?"

"Yeah," I admitted.

"I see. Why do you feel this need to be silly all the time?"

"It's not a need," I explained. "Something about Earth's atmosphere gave me a superior

sense of humor. Even if I try, I can't stop making jokes."

"I see. And that yellow cape," she continued. "Why do you wear it?"

"Because my other yellow cape is in the wash."

"I see," Dr. Breznitski said, taking notes. "I'd

like you to look at this picture and tell me what you see."

She handed me a card with a black-and-white drawing on it. I looked at it carefully.

"It's an Eskimo girl ice fishing outside her igloo," I reported.

Dr. Breznitski had a puzzled look on her face. She leaned over to check the drawing.

"There's no Eskimo girl," she said. "There's no igloo. It's a picture of a boy throwing a rock. Why did you say you saw an Eskimo girl ice fishing outside her igloo?"

"The Eskimo girl is *behind* the boy throwing the rock," I explained.

"How do you know there's an Eskimo girl behind the boy throwing the rock?"

"I *didn't* know," I said. "You just told me."

"I see," Dr. Breznitski said, a little flustered. "But let's focus on the boy throwing the rock. What's he throwing the rock at? His father, perhaps?"

"No, a polar bear," I said.

"What polar bear?!" Dr. Breznitski asked, raising her voice a little.

"The polar bear behind the Eskimo girl," I explained.

"Forget about the picture," Dr. Breznitski said, snatching the card away from me and fumbling for something in her desk drawer. "I'd like you to play with these wooden blocks. I'll watch. Be creative. Just do whatever you want with them."

I took one of the wooden blocks, put it in my mouth, and ate it.

"What are you, crazy?!" Dr. Breznitski screamed. "Why did you do that?"

"I'm having a snack," I said, munching the block.

"Do you have any idea how much those blocks cost?"

"You *told* me to do whatever I want with them," I said.

"I didn't think you were going to *eat* them!"

"If you didn't want me to eat them, you shouldn't have told me to do whatever I wanted with them."

Dr. Breznitski pulled out a handkerchief and mopped her forehead with it.

"I'm sorry," she told me, getting up and walking to the door. "They never prepared me for a situation like this in graduate school."

"No problem," I said. "Hey, those blocks are good. Can I have another one?"

She rushed out of the office and came back in,

this time with Bob Foster. He said hi and took the seat next to mine.

"Mr. Foster," the doctor explained, "I've done some tests with Funny Boy and come to the conclusion that he suffers from a very rare psychological disorder."

Bob Foster leaned forward in his seat, a concerned look on his face.

"What is it, doctor?"

"Funnyitis," Dr. Breznitski explained. "The complete inability to take anything seriously."

"Will you have to amputate my head?" I asked.

"See what I mean?" Dr. Breznitski said.

"Is there a cure, doctor?" asked Bob Foster.

"Sadly, no," Dr. Breznitski explained. "But we may be able to keep it under control."

"How?" Bob Foster asked. "With medication?"

"No," Dr. Breznitski explained. "The only effective treatment for funnyitis is bombarding the child with very serious and unexciting stimuli. Doing this, we hope to neutralize the part of his brain that responds to humor."

"So what should I do for him, Doctor?"

"Have him watch golf tournaments on television," Dr. Breznitski suggested. "Also, try the Food Network. Expose him to foreign films. Newbery Award–winning books. Things like that. Whatever you do, make sure you keep him away from anything that is amusing or entertaining in any way."

"What about when he grows up?" Bob Foster asked the doctor. "Will he be able to lead a normal life?"

"It's hard to say," the doctor replied. "Some sufferers of funnyitis become stand-up comics. More likely he will become one of those annoying adults who makes a dumb joke no matter what you say to them. It's a sad, pathetic life, but at least he isn't likely to hurt anyone."

Dr. Breznitski got up from her chair, which I guess was her signal that we should leave. Bob Foster and I got up, too.

"Begin treatment tonight," the doctor suggested. "I want him to watch two hours of the Weather Channel. If he finds anything funny, call 911."

I'd had enough. I was sick of people testing me

and asking me questions and deciding what was wrong with me.

"There's nothing wrong with me!" I shouted. "You're the crazy ones! I've got to save the world!"

"Save the world?" Dr. Breznitski laughed. "From what?"

"Those barbers! They're going to take everybody's hair and flush it down the drain, cutting off our water supply!"

"Are you referring to Bo, Barry, and Burly?" Dr. Breznitski said. "That's my favorite show."

"Hey, mine, too!" Bob Foster added.

"It's not a show!" I screamed. "It's for real!"

Dr. Breznitski shook her head sadly and leaned toward Bob Foster. "One of the most obvious signs of funnyitis," she whispered, "is that the patient finds humor in everything *except* things that other people consider funny. Baffling, isn't it?"

I ran all the way home.

Chapter 9

HAIR TO THE CHIEF

That night, the Weather Channel was showing a two-hour special on the history of the thermometer. Bob Foster forced me to watch it. After fifteen minutes, I thought I was going to jump out of my skin. Punch was asleep on the floor.

"Turn it off," I begged Bob Foster. "Please, turn it off!"

"The doctor said you had to watch for two hours."

Fortunately, at that moment, the phone rang. I jumped up to get it before Bob Foster could. I just wanted to get away from the TV.

"Is this Funny Boy?" a woman asked.

"Yes."

"Please hold a moment for the President of the United States."

"Yeah, sure," I said to the lady. "I told you people to stop calling us! How many times do I have to tell you I don't buy things from people who call over the phone?"

But she was gone. There was a click on the line, and then . . .

"Funny Boy! It's me, the President. I need to see you right away in Washington."

The President of the United States! The real President of the United States was calling *me*. It was the most exciting moment of my life. My heart was pounding.

73

"I'm kinda busy," I told the President. "How about Wednesday?"

"Earth may be destroyed by Wednesday!"

Wow, I thought. If Earth could be destroyed by Wednesday, I wouldn't have to take Punch to the vet. That's great because she hates going to the vet. And if Earth could be destroyed by Wednesday, Bob Foster wouldn't have to pay his bills. There would be no reason to wash his car either, because if Earth was destroyed, there would be no roads to drive on. And besides, the car wouldn't exist anymore.

This was terrific news! I wouldn't have to pick up the newspaper from the front lawn in the morning, because if Earth was going to be destroyed, nobody would read the paper because all life would be destroyed and we'd all be dead and—

"I'll be on the next plane to Washington," I told the President.

The first thing in the morning, Bob Foster, Punch, and I went to the airport to catch a plane to Washington. Punch was really angry that we had to put her into one of those dog carriers, but rules are rules.

A limousine picked us up at the Washington airport and whisked us to the White House. A woman with gray hair was waiting at the front gate.

"Who's the old bag?" I asked as the limousine pulled up.

"Show some respect," Bob Foster replied. "That's the first lady."

"She can't be *that* old!" I exclaimed. "There must have been at least one lady before her."

"The first lady is the President's wife!"

Bob Foster, Punch, and I got out of the limo.

"It is a pleasure to meet you," Bob Foster said gracefully. The first lady looked me up and down, like she'd never seen a boy wearing a cape and fake nose and glasses before.

"He's fictional," Punch informed her.

The first lady stepped back in surprise.

"Your dog . . . " she said. "She . . . talks?"

"I can also sing the theme song to *The Brady Bunch*," Punch told her. "Wanna hear it?"

"That won't be necessary."

The first lady led us to the Oval Office, where the President works. When she opened the door, he was nervously pacing around the room.

"Funny Boy!" he exclaimed as soon as he saw me. "Finally, you're here! Remember how you defeated that airsick alien from Andromeda who threatened to eat Earth one continent at a time?"

"Yes."

"Well, I need your help again."

The President motioned us to sit. Then he sat behind his desk, put his head in his hands, and started sobbing.

"What's the matter, Mr. President?" Bob Foster asked.

"I don't want to lose my hair!" the President whimpered.

"Your hair?" we all asked.

"I've always had good hair," the President exclaimed. "That's how I got elected in the first place."

"I thought you got elected because the American people carefully evaluated the issues and decided they agreed with your policies," I said.

"They felt you were the best man to lead the country."

"No, no, no!" he sobbed. "That had nothing to do with it. It was just my great hair!"

"Are you suggesting that those kooky barbers on TV are for *real*?" Bob Foster asked.

"That's what I've been trying to tell you!" I said. "They're going to take our hair, and then they're going to take over."

The President began wailing, big tears sliding down his cheeks.

"Get a grip on yourself, sir," I told him. "It's just hair."

"Just hair?" the President said, pulling himself together. "Young man, do you have any idea how important hair is?"

"I guess not."

"Do you know why Columbus sailed to America?"

"He wanted to reach the New World?" I guessed.

"No," the President explained. "He couldn't get a good haircut in Spain."

"What about the Barber of Seville?" I asked, but the President ignored me.

"Do you know what causes high tide and low tide?" he asked.

"The moon, I think."

"No," the President replied. "That's just what we *tell* everybody. Actually, it's hair. And do you know what makes the stock market go up and down?"

"Uh . . . hair?"

"Exactly!"

"Gee, I had no idea that hair was so important."

"Young man, you don't know the half of it. Hair makes the world go 'round. Without hair we are nothing. You know what is the biggest difference between human beings and the animal world?"

"Humans have thumbs?" Punch guessed.

"No."

"Humans can think and reason?" Bob Foster guessed.

"No."

"Humans have a sense of humor?" I guessed.

"No!" the President thundered. "Humans have hair!"

"Animals have hair, too," Punch pointed out. "See? Look at mine."

"Don't interrupt me!" the President said. "Funny Boy, if not for hair, we'd all be . . . bald. It's up to you to save the hair, I mean the world. You're our only hope against these loony barbers."

"Can't you just drop bombs on them?" Bob Foster asked.

"What am I going to say to the Air Force? Go drop bombs on those three barbers who have the highest rated television show in history? The press would laugh at me. I can see the head-lines—PREZ FLIPS WIG. HAIR WAR BEGINS."

He had a point, I had to admit.

"I had no choice but to call on you," the President said seriously. "My hands are tied. Our

backs are against the wall. They've got us right where they want us. It's now or never. Do or die. It's time to see what we're made of. The fate of Earth is in your hands. Did I leave out any clichés?"

"I believe you forgot 'when the going gets tough, the tough get going,' sir," Bob Foster said.

"Oh yeah," said the President. "When the going gets tough, the tough get going."

"Mr. President," I said. "I won't let you down, sir. They haven't got a hair. I mean, they haven't got a prayer."

"I knew I could count on you," the President said as he walked us to the door of the Oval Office.

"I'll get to the root of the problem, sir."

"Funny Boy," the President said solemnly, "this could get hairy."

Chapter 10

BAD HAIR DAY FOR EARTH!

When Bob Foster, Punch, and I left the White House after our meeting with the President, I felt excited . . . and worried. "The fate of Earth is in your hands," the President had told me. It was an awesome responsibility.

"I'm sorry that I doubted you," Bob told me as we got into the limo. "I thought those barbers were just a new comedy show."

"That's what everybody thinks, Dad. Now you know the truth."

"What's your plan to stop them?"

"I'll defeat them with humor," I replied grimly. "Once they hear my jokes, they'll surrender and go back where they came from."

"But your jokes stink," Punch said.

"Then I'll have to get new ones."

We returned home and gathered around Bob's computer. He logged on to the Internet and did a search for "jokes." In seconds, we had a list of hundreds of joke Web sites put together by people who have entirely too much time on their hands.

There were riddles, limericks, and puns. Animal jokes. Mommy-mommy jokes. Lightbulb jokes. Lawyer jokes. Knock-knock jokes. Clean jokes and

dirty jokes. Long jokes and one-liners. The list was endless. We stayed up all night going through them until we had an inventory of can't miss, fall-on-the-floor, laugh-out-loud knee-slappers.

We were ready to do battle.

A government plane rushed us to the barbers' headquarters at a secret location on the Barbary Coast, on the African shores of the Mediterranean Sea. As official representatives of the President, we were immediately taken to the barbers.

A door opened and we were ushered into a large room. There was a map of the world on one wall, with some of the countries colored in red. Three big barber chairs were in the middle of the room, facing away from us. One side of the room was filled with big plastic trash bags.

"Hair," Bob Foster whispered to me. "Bags and bags of hair."

Suddenly the three barber chairs swiveled around, and there they were. Bo, Barry, and Burly Barber. They looked just like they looked on TV, only meaner and uglier. Their toupees were crooked.

For a moment, they glared at us in silence. I trembled. I felt like we were meeting the great and powerful Oz.

"D-d-don't worry," Punch whispered to me. "They're fictional, like us."

"Shut up, Punch."

"Who speaks?" Burly Barber thundered. "The dog? What is it you want?"

"Uh . . ." Punch stammered. "I love your TV show. Can I have your autographs?"

"Shut up, Punch," I said.

"Me torture them, okay, boss?" Bo Barber said.

"Not yet," Barry Barber said. "They're just in time. We are about to start shooting tonight's episode."

"Oh yeah?" I said, stepping forward boldly. "Well, *The Bo, Barry, and Burly Show* is canceled. Starting right now."

"Who is it who speaks in a rude manner?" Burly Barber boomed.

"I am Funny Boy," I announced. "I have been sent by the President of the United States to defend the planet Earth, including some parts of

New Jersey that nobody in their right mind would ever want to visit. That is my duty."

"Him say doody!" Bo Barber smirked.

"Not doody," I corrected him. "*Duty*."

The author wishes to personally apologize at this point for making that cheap and revolting toilet joke. It won't happen again. Unless he thinks up another one.

"Sometimes," Barry Barber said thoughtfully, "two words in English sound the same but have different spellings and different meanings. That is another reason why we must destroy Earth! To end this senseless confusion. Right, my brothers?"

Bo and Burly Barber nodded their heads in agreement.

"Look," Bob Foster said. "Why are you barbers so mad? Earth is a very nice place. Something must have happened to you a long time ago to make you so mean and angry."

"You speak the truth, tan man," Barry Barber agreed. "It all started with the Big Bang."

WARNING TO READER: If you read the following paragraph, you may actually learn something. If you are reading this book purely for laughs, please—we beg you—please do not read the next paragraph!

The Big Bang was an enormous fiery explosion of hydrogen atoms that some scientists believe created the universe ten billion years ago. According to the theory, the universe expanded rapidly after the Big Bang. It cooled enough in one million years for atoms to form, and eventually, living creatures.

"Our home planet, Depilatory, is far beyond your galaxy," Barry Barber explained. "Depilatory existed millions of years before your Earth. Our people were minding their own business when suddenly the Big Bang took place. The force of the explosion was so powerful that it blew the hair off every man, woman, and child on Depilatory."

"Hair never grow back," Bo said sadly, and then he began to cry.

"That was billions of years ago!" I exclaimed. "Isn't it time you people got over it?"

"Depilatorians have long memories," Barry replied.

"Let me ask you a question," Bob Foster said. "If the people on your planet haven't had any hair since the Big Bang, why did the three of you decide to become barbers?"

"There was very little competition," Barry said.

Bob Foster leaned over and whispered to me. "On their planet, these three guys are losers."

"I don't get it," I said. "Your hair was blown off in the Big Bang and you're still mad. Fine. Why take it out on the people of Earth? Earthlings never did anything to you."

"No, but Earthlings can do something *for* us," Barry Barber said. "We scanned the galaxies looking for a planet that had the essential ingredient Depilatorians need to exist—hair. There is enough hair here on Earth to cover the head of every Depilatorian for the next hundred years."

"So you decided to take our hair and bring it home with you," Bob Foster said.

"Exactly."

"Me be hero!" Burly Barber said proudly.

"How about bringing home some souvenir T-shirts instead?" I suggested. You know: "MY BARBER VISITED EARTH AND ALL HE GOT ME WAS THIS STUPID T-SHIRT."

"Me no want T-shirt!" Bo Barber bellowed. "Me want hair!"

"Why don't you just wear hats?" asked Punch.

"Enough small talk!" Barry Barber announced. "We have come for your hair and we will leave with your hair!"

"What makes you think you can get away

with this?" Bob Foster asked. "We have smart bombs, tanks, nuclear weapons, laser-guided missiles . . ."

"Haha!" Bo Barber chuckled. "Toys."

"Oh yeah," I said. "What weapons do *you* have?

"We don't need weapons," Barry informed us. "We will make you choke on your own hair! We won't have to fire a shot! Hahahaha!"

The other two barbers joined in the laughter. Bob Foster, Punch, and I looked at each other. These barbers were really out of their minds.

"This is our plan," Barry Barber said. "Using our hair guns, we will take your hair and send half of it back to the grateful citizens of Depilatory on a rocket. We will be heroes in our homeland. Then we will take the other half of the hair and shove it down your showers and toilets and sinks. This will clog up your drains and pipes until your water supply is entirely cut off."

"Where can I get one of those hair guns?" asked Punch.

"Shut up, Punch."

"When you turn on your faucets and nothing comes out, you'll surrender," Barry said gleefully.

"And if you don't, the buildup of water in your pipes will cause an explosion that will blow Earth into pieces the size of M&M's!"

"Bad hair day for Earth!" proclaimed Bo Barber.

"Hahahahaha!" all three barbers chortled gleefully.

"Good plan, yes?" asked Burly Barber.

"That's the stupidest harebrained plan I ever heard in my life," I replied.

"Who ask you, big-nose boy?"

"You did," I said. "Look, I'll make a deal with you. Surrender now, and we'll change the name of the George Washington Bridge to the Bo,

Barry, and Burly Bridge. How would you like that?"

"Me no want stinking bridge!" Bo Barber barked. "Me want hair!"

"Well, we're not going to give it to you," I said.

"How will you," Barry Barber asked, "a mere boy, stop us from carrying out our plan? Do you have some super power, or something?"

"It just so happens that I do," I explained. "I have a superior sense of humor. It can reduce anyone, human or alien, into helpless chuckling. Giggles come next. Then guffaws and chortles set in. Finally, unless you surrender, you will die laughing. That is how I will defeat you."

"Me no laugh," Burly Barber insisted.

"Me no laugh, too," agreed Bo Barber.

"Everyone laughs," I said. "A smile is the universal language. And it's impossible to do evil and laugh at the same time."

"I defy you!" Barry challenged. "Try to make us laugh."

"Okay," I said. "How many ears did Davy Crockett have?"

"Me not know."

"Three," I said. "His left ear, his right ear, and his wild front ear."

They stared at me.

"Get it?" Punch asked. Then she sang, "Davy Crockett, king of the wild frontier . . ."

"Me no get it."

"These guys are really dumb," Bob Foster whispered. "Try something simpler."

"Okay," I said. "Why don't cannibals eat clowns?"

"Me not know," Bo Barber said.

"They taste funny."

Bo Barber and his brother barbers just stared. Bob Foster leaned over to me.

"Maybe they can't relate to these jokes. Have you got anything about hair?"

"Good idea," I said. "What kind of hair do oceans have?"

"Me not know."

"Wavy hair," I replied. "Get it?"

Nothing. Not even a smile. These barbers were *tough*!

"You not funny," Burly Barber said, taking a step toward me.

"Him be funnier bald," Burly Barber said, reaching behind his back for something.

"It's the hair gun!" Punch shouted.

"Let's get out of here!" Bob Foster exclaimed.

He didn't have to tell me twice. I wasn't about to stick around and let some nutty barber point that thing at me. I ran for the door. Bob Foster was right in front of me, and Punch was at my heels.

"Run for it!" I yelled as we dove out the door.

"We'll get you, Funny Boy," yelled Barry, "and your little dog, too!"

We made a dash for it and we didn't stop running until we were safely out of there. I reached up and ran my hand across my head. My hair was still there.

"Where's Punch?" I asked Bob Foster.

"I thought she was with you."

Suddenly, Punch came scampering over. She looked okay, but as she got closer I could see that . . . *she had no hair*!

I don't know if you've ever seen a cocker spaniel that has been totally shaved, but it's not a

pretty sight. It's amazing how much of a dog is just hair. Without her fur coat, Punch looked like a starved rat.

"Punch!" I shouted. "Are you okay?"

"Do I *look* okay?" Punch said sarcastically. "Look at me! I might as well be a Mexican hairless! I can't walk down the street like this! I'll be the laughingstock of the whole animal kingdom."

After a while, Bob Foster and I were able to calm Punch down. The limousine took us back to the airport. A plane was waiting to take us home.

I was glad we were safe, but I felt terrible at the same time. Our mission had been a failure. I hadn't stopped the barbers. I had let down my President. I had let down my adopted world.

"Why did you run away?" Punch asked me once our plane was in the air. Bob Foster was sitting a few rows away.

"I couldn't defeat them," I explained sadly. "It was hopeless. I told them joke after joke and they didn't crack a smile."

"You can't give up," Punch said. "You're Funny Boy! You're the funniest kid on the planet. Never forget that."

"They're too tough," I moaned. "Those guys wouldn't laugh if their lives depended on it."

Unfortunately, it was *our* lives that depended on it. I spent the rest of the flight staring out the window. I was a failure. For once, I didn't feel funny at all.

If your dad tells you to go to bed this instant, don't stop reading. It's more important for you to finish this book than it is for you to sleep.

Chapter 11

PATHETIC EARTHLINGS ALLOW THE BARBERS TO EXECUTE THEIR DIABOLICAL PLAN WITHOUT PUTTING UP A FIGHT

Every night that week, we gathered in the living room so I could watch whatever was on the Weather Channel. Usually, it was the weather.

"Why is there a channel for weather?" I asked Bob Foster. "Can't people just look outside and see what the weather is?"

"The Weather Channel is supposed to cure you of funnyitis," Bob Foster said. "It's working, too. I've noticed you don't crack nearly as many jokes as you used to."

He was right about that. Ever since my miserable confrontation with the nutty barbers, nothing seemed very funny to me. But the Weather Channel had nothing to do with it. I was just depressed.

When two hours were up, Bob Foster would tune in *The Bo, Barry, and Burly Show*. He said it was okay for me to laugh, but I never did.

By now, the three barbers were a worldwide sensation. They were on the cover of every magazine. There were rumors about a Bo, Barry, and Burly movie in the works, a Bo, Barry, and Burly book, a Bo, Barry, and Burly cartoon series.

Every night, we would watch as Bo, Barry, and Burly removed the hair of another nation. Spain. Egypt. Germany. China. The barbers were moving across the globe. One by one, people all over the world were going bald.

And here in America, everybody still thought it was a big joke. Articles like this one were in the paper every day . . . .

CHINA JUMPS ON BALD FAD!

The entire nation of China went bald today, demonstrating the incredible popularity "The Bo, Barry, and Burly Show" has in Asia. People all over the world love these wacky barbers so much they are shaving their heads so they will resemble their heroes. Being bald is the hottest trend.

"It is the coolest look," said Zang Chen of Shanghai. "And I save a lot of money on shampoo!"

One billion Chinese can't be wrong, can they?

Little by little, the barbers were removing the hair of the human race. And nobody seemed to care. I couldn't do anything about it. I felt so helpless. My sense of humor was slipping away.

In school, Mrs. Wonderland couldn't have been happier at the change that had come over me.

"I'm just amazed at the improvement in your behavior!" she gushed one morning before school started. "No more silly jokes while I'm trying to teach the class. No more pranks, remarks, or dumb riddles. It's like you're an entirely different child! I can see that Dr. Breznitski's therapy is working. I just might have the whole class watch the Weather Channel!"

I lumbered to my desk and sat down heavily. Maybe the world was going to be destroyed, but as long as I was serious and not making jokes in class, Mrs. Wonderland was thrilled.

"Hey, doofus!" Salvatore whispered to me. "Whatsa matter with you? You ain't told none of your feeble jokes in a long time."

"I just don't feel like it," I answered weakly.

I felt even worse the next day. The kids had talked Mrs. Wonderland into having a Bo, Barry, and Burly Day at school. I walked in that morning and everyone in the class was wearing baldy wigs.

Not only that, but they brought in all kinds of Bo, Barry and Burly stuff for show and share. Bo, Barry, and Burly backpacks and T-shirts. Bo,

Barry, and Burly trading cards and magazines. Bo, Barry, and Burly Beanie Babies. It was revolting.

Even Salvatore got into it. He brought in his talking Bo, Barry, and Burly action figures. When you squeeze their hands, they say catchphrases like "Give me your hair, or die!" and "Soon the entire Earth will be bald, bald, bald!"

All the kids were laughing, high-fiving each other, and having a great time. They were clueless. I couldn't believe the people of Earth were just letting these insane barbers take over without a fight.

An announcement came over the loudspeaker that we should all rise and recite the pledge of allegiance.

"I pledge allegiance to the flag of the United States of America . . . "

I had to do something, I thought to myself. I was Funny Boy, wasn't I?

"And to the Republic for which it stands . . . "

It was my duty to protect Earth, wasn't it? If I didn't act, nobody else would.

"One nation under God, indivisible, with liberty and justice for all."

I bolted out of the classroom.

"Hey, I didn't say you could leave the room!" Mrs. Wonderland hollered at me. "Where do you think you're going?"

"To save the world!"

Chapter 12

AND NOW, FUNNY BOY, IT IS TIME FOR YOU TO DIE!

The President had put planes, helicopters, and limousines at my disposal so I could get to the barbers at a moment's notice. Fortunately, I wouldn't have to go far. I called the White House and the President told me that the barbers were now in Toronto, Canada.

"They've already removed most of the world's hair," the President said mournfully. "North and South America are all that is left."

"They're going to pay for this!" I said. "Get it? To pay? Toupee?"

"You'll need to be a lot funnier than that, Funny Boy," the President replied. "You're our last hope."

The seriousness of my mission had hit home

with me. I was starting to feel funny again. Jokes were welling up inside my brain, ready to burst out and reduce even the most serious villian into a convulsion of giggles.

I called Bob Foster at work and he rushed home. We put Punch in her little cage and took a government jet to Toronto. From there, it was minutes by limousine to the Sky Dome, where the Toronto Blue Jays baseball team plays. It was also where Bo, Barry, and Burly Barber had set up their North American headquarters.

Bob Foster, Punch, and I marched inside the Sky Dome. It was an enormous stadium. But it wasn't the field that caught our attention. It was the huge barber pole at second base that reached almost to the roof. I had been to the National Air and Space Museum in Washington, D.C., but I had never seen a rocket so big.

This was the spaceship I had seen through the telescope. It was probably filled with hair and ready for launch, Bob Foster whispered to me. Stolen hair. Once they shipped the hair back to Depilatory, they would be heroes to their people.

I spotted Bo, Barry, and Burly at the bottom of

the rocket, tinkering with switches and dials.

"Halt, hair thieves!" I shouted.

"Well, if it isn't Funny Boy and Tan Man!" Barry Barber said, almost gleefully. "We meet again. Your little dog looks kind of cute without its fur coat."

"Your hair-robbing days are over!" Punch shouted.

"Me torture them, okay, boss?" Bo Barber asked.

"Not yet," Barry Barber said. "First, let them

watch as we remove the hair of every Canadian citizen. And when we're done, the United States will have its turn. Then we will flush enough hair down the drains of North America to blow this planet to smithereens!"

"Hahahaha!" the three barbers guffawed.

"I'll give you one last chance," I said, trying to remain calm. "Surrender now and leave Earth alone. Go quietly and you won't be punished so severely for your crimes."

"Why should we?" Barry Barber asked, defiantly.

"If you don't, I will tell a joke that is so funny that you will fall to the ground, helpless with laughter. You will be totally unable to perform your evil deeds. You'll be lucky you don't cough up your appendix or some other internal organ."

"Ha!" snorted Burly Barber. "Me hear that last time. Me dare you. Make Burly laugh."

"Who's dumb and flies a plane?" I asked.

"Me not know."

"Amelia Airhead."

The three barbers looked at each other.

"That's *it*?" Barry Barber asked. "*That's* the

joke that was going to make us fall over dead?"

"That was just his warm-up joke," Punch explained. "Now he's going to tell you the real joke. Right, Funny Boy?"

"Uh, right."

I felt sweat beading up on my forehead. The Amelia Airhead joke was the best one I had. I would have to come up with a good one right here or it would be good-bye Earth.

"Here comes the real joke," I continued. "This centipede walks into a shoe store—"

"Enough!" bellowed Barry Barber. "Seize them!"

Bo and Burly grabbed Bob Foster, Punch and me. They strapped us into the three barber chairs.

"You'll never get away with this!" Bob Foster shouted. "NATO forces will track you down and bring you to justice!"

"Me not *think* so," Bo Barber said, smiling his evil smile.

"After we clog all your drains with hair," Barry Barber explained, "we will dump tons of shampoo into your oceans. Your waters will be filled with foamy white lather, making it impossible for ships to find us. Then we will surround Earth with a cloud of talcum powder, making it impossible for airplanes to find us. Escape will be simple. Hahahaha!"

"You're madmen!" Punch yelled.

"Thank you!" Burly Barber grunted.

I tried to free my hands from the straps that were holding me in the barber chair, but it was impossible.

"Do something!" I yelled to Punch.

"Like what?"

"Growl! Bare your teeth or something!"

"Baring teeth is so . . . animalistic!"

"You're an animal!" I screamed. Ever since Punch discovered she could talk, she refused to lower herself to things she considered "doglike."

"Why don't *you* do something?" Punch said. "Tell a joke. You're Funny Boy!"

I tried to think of a joke, any joke. Nothing came to mind.

"I . . . I can't think of one!" I replied.

"What do you mean?" Punch yelled. "You know *hundreds* of jokes. Night and day you're always telling your stupid jokes. And now, now when we really need it, you can't think of a single joke?"

"My mind is a blank!" I moaned.

Bob Foster tried to bail us out. "Be sensible," he implored the barbers. "On Earth, you guys are superstars. You've got the number one show on TV. You could be bigger than the Beatles. Why destroy Earth and go back to your planet, where you guys have no jobs, no lives?"

"Silence!" Barry Barber boomed. "We must warm up the hair-removal generator."

"Wait!" I shouted desperately. "Aren't you

HAIR REMOVAL
GENERATOR
BDR-529

going to give us a last request? Even a con-
demned man gets one last request."

"What is your last request?" Barry said grudg-
ingly.

"I want to make a phone call."

"All right," Barry said, handing me a cell
phone. "But don't try any funny stuff."

Fumbling with the buttons, I punched in the
number for Dial-a-Joke. In seconds, I had what I
needed.

"Why do seagulls fly over the sea?" I shouted
at the barbers.

"Me not know."

"If they flew over the bay, they'd be bagels."

Barry Barber ripped the phone from my hand.
"I said no funny stuff! You're beginning to get on
my nerves."

"Me say shoot him," Burly Barber suggested.

"No," Barry Barber replied. "I have a better
idea."

He reached into his back pocket and pulled
out a battery-operated hair clipper, the kind barbers use to trim sideburns. He turned it on, and
it made a loud buzzing noise.

"I'm going to remove Funny Boy's hair *personally*!"

"No," I shrieked. "Stop! Stop!"

It was no use. He was too strong. He took the clipper and ran it right down the middle of my scalp. Hair went flying everywhere. Down my back. In my eyes. It was horrible.

When he was done, I ran my fingers across the top of my head. There was nothing there but skin. He had cut a straight strip right across the middle, like a farmer who plowed a row of a field. I had a negative Mohawk.

"You're not barbers!" I screamed. "You're . . . barbarians!"

"Yes, we are," agreed Barry. "And now it is time for you to die!"

So how are you enjoying the story so far? Exciting, isn't it? Do you think Funny Boy can escape from these bubble-brained barbers? Or is it all over for him? What about Punch? Will her hair grow back? Will Bob Foster lose his job at the underwear factory? Does Principal Werner really kill children and eat them?

You know that you're almost at the end of the story, because there are only a few pages left in this book. We thought we could build the suspense by forcing you to read this meaningless stuff before revealing the ending. Pretty clever, huh? It pads the book out a little, too. We know you're already sick of this. Well, too bad, you have to read the whole thing.

Okay, okay, back to the story . . .

Chapter 13

THE BIG SURPRISE ENDING THAT WILL COMPLETELY SHOCK YOU, UNLESS YOU'VE ALREADY GUESSED IT

So like I was saying, Bob Foster, Punch, and I were strapped to barber chairs in the middle of the Toronto Sky Dome. The loony barbers had just cut a swath of my hair out right down the middle of my head. Barry Barber had this evil grin on his face, and I had the feeling he was going to do some other terrible thing to me.

"Do you still think we're fictional characters?" I asked Punch.

"I'm not so sure anymore," Punch replied. "But your fictional hair is all over the floor."

"Enough chitchat, Funny Boy!" Barry Barber said. "Now it is time for you to die!"

"You're going to kill me?"

"Not D-I-E, you idiot!" Barry said. "Dye! D-Y-E. We're going to dye your hair . . . purple!"

"Why?" I asked.

"Because purple is my favorite color."

Purple is my favorite color. That's it! The word "color" sparked something in the farthest corners of my memory. Jokes started flooding into my brain.

"Speaking of the color purple," I said, "what's the difference between a grape and a chicken?"

"Me not know," Bo Barber said.

"They're both purple, except for the chicken."

"Please stop that," Barry said. "It's annoying."

"More jokes!" Punch shouted. "Quickly!"

"What's red and shaped like a bucket?" I asked.

"Me not know."

"A red bucket!"

"Please!" Barry moaned. "Nobody wants to listen to that. You're giving me a headache."

"Tell another one!" Bob Foster yelled.

"What's black, white, and a zebra?" I asked.

"Me not know."

"A zebra!"

"Ugh!" Barry said. "How does he do it? Just when I think he has told the worst joke in history, he comes out with one that's even less funny than the one before!"

"Ask me if I'm an orange," I commanded them.

"Are you an orange?"

"No!" I replied.

"Ugh!" Barry Barber moaned. "I think my head is going to explode if I have to listen to one more of these."

"What's pink and fluffy?"

"Me not know."

"Pink fluff!"

"My brains hurt!" moaned Bo Barber. "My brains hurt."

"No more," Burly Barber groaned, holding his hands over his ears. "Me do anything! No more stupid jokes!"

"Okay," I said. "I want the three of you lunatics out of here. Understand? Hop on the next barber pole heading for Delipatory and never come back. You read me?"

"No!" Barry Barber shouted suddenly. He took a handkerchief out of his pocket and rolled it up. Then he wrapped it around my head so it covered my mouth. He tied it tightly.

"That ought to shut him up," Barry said.

"But it won't shut *me* up!" came a voice from behind us.

"Who said that?" Bob Foster asked.

I turned around.

It was Salvatore, that big guy in my class at school! The three barbers shrank back in fear.

"Salvatore!" I shouted, after he cut me loose

with his pocket knife. "What are *you* doing here?"

"I had to save you," he explained. "Mrs. Wonderland always hated me. Then you came into the class telling those dumb jokes, and she hated you even more. She left me alone for a while. But then you got all depressed and stopped telling jokes, so Mrs. Wonderland got on my case again. I have to bring you back so you can tell more jokes at school. It's the only way I'll ever make it out of fourth grade."

"But how did you get to Toronto?"

"I stowed away on your limo and your plane," Salvatore said.

What a pal!

"I've got a joke, too," Salvatore said to the cowering barbers. "Who is big and strong and is going to hurt you?"

"Me not know."

"I am!" Salvatore announced, raising his fist. "Now scram before I turn you into shredded wheat."

The three barbers started running toward their spaceship so fast, their toupees fell off.

"See?" Punch said. "I told you everything would turn out okay in the end. It always does in these fictional stories."

"That was a close shave," I said.

After It Was All Over . . .

Well, once again I have conquered the forces of evil. I couldn't have done it on my own. With you doing the reading and me hitting those creepy barbers with my jokes, goodness and niceness have prevailed.

Together, we have made the world safe. Safe for individually wrapped slices of cheese. Safe for WrestleMania and Mr. Potato Head. Safe for talking toys that start talking in the middle of the night when you're trying to sleep. Safe for Slim Jims and junk E-mail and Kmart.

As a gesture of goodwill, I walked over to the spaceship on the launchpad. Bo, Barry, and Burly were just about to get on board. They looked depressed and defeated.

"To show you I have no hard feelings," I told them, "I would like to give you a small gift to take back to Delipatory."

I took a red plastic comb out of my pocket and handed it to Barry Barber.

"A comb?" he asked, puzzled. "Why are you giving us this? Everyone on our planet is bald. What are we going to do with a comb?"

"I wanted to give you something you would never part with," I said.

Barry Barber looked at me.

"It's a joke!" I exclaimed. "Get it? Never part with?"

"Get inside the ship!" Barry Barber shouted to his brothers. "Quickly! He'll never stop telling those awful jokes!"

"Me get out of this place!" Bo shouted as he slammed the hatch behind him.

"Wait!" I hollered, pounding on the side of the ship. "I just thought of some more jokes to tell you."

The engine fired up and a huge roar echoed off the sides of the Sky Dome. I backed away as flames shot out the bottom of the barber pole.

Slowly, the pole rose off the ground. Bob Foster, Punch, Salvatore, and I waved as it gained speed and rocketed into the sky.

"Some folks," I said, "just can't take a joke."

Naturally, none of what you just read made the news. The government was careful not to let the public know how close Earth had come to being destroyed. *The Bo, Barry, and Burly Show* was on TV that night as scheduled, with three actors pretending to be Bo, Barry, and Burly. Nobody knew the difference.

When I went to school the next day, there was no banner welcoming me back as a conquering hero. Salvatore threw me a wink, but nobody congratulated me or thanked me for what I had done.

"You're late!" Mrs. Wonderland snapped when I walked through the door. "Where's your homework?"

"I didn't do it," I admitted. "I was busy saving the world."

"Is that the best excuse you can come up with?" Mrs. Wonderland replied wearily. "I'm really not in the mood for your foolishness today."

"Mood?" I said. "Speaking of mood, what do cows get when they're sick?"

"What?"

"Hay fever!"

"Go to Principal Werner's office!" she shouted.

"Way to go, dork!" Salvatore said as I passed his desk. He stuck out his hand and I slapped it.

Well, that concludes this adventure. Until we meet again, my friends, I leave you with one small piece of wisdom. A laugh, which brings so much happiness to the world, is merely the sudden discharge of air from the body. And so is blowing your nose, sneezing, belching, coughing, and farting.

Okay, you can stop reading now.

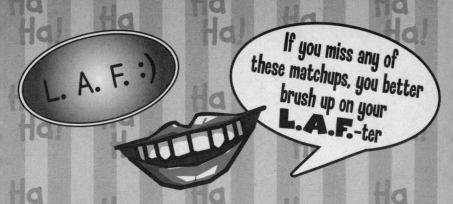

L. A. F. :)

If you miss any of these matchups, you better brush up on your **L.A.F.**-ter

MATCH THE CHARACTER TO THE L.A.F. BOOK

1. Stan from Pan
2. Perfect Peter
3. Punch
4. Trudie

a. *Horrid Henry*
b. *Funny Boy*
c. *Lab Coat Girl*
d. *Nose Pickers*

ANSWERS: 1. d; 2. a; 3. b; 4. c